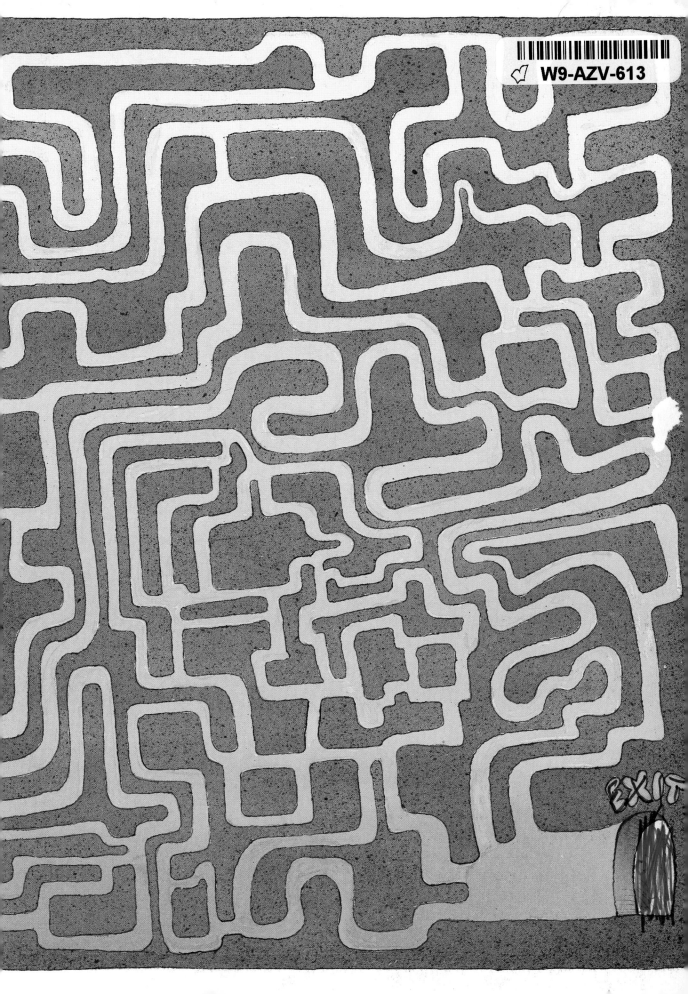

W9-AZV-613

EXIT

NISHU

First published in USA 1987
by Exeter Books
Distributed by Bookthrift
Exeter is a trademark of Bookthrift Marketing, Inc.
Bookthrift is a registered trademark of Bookthrift Marketing, Inc.
New York, New York

ISBN 0 671 08180 2

Printed in Hong Kong
by Imago Publishing Ltd.

KORKY!

# THE BRAINBOX

## story by Keren Kristal

Exeter Books

NEW YORK

". . . . . . Now dear, open your presents."

I ran to my presents, which were piled high next to my birthday cake. Just in time, I caught the top one as it wobbled over. I snatched it up. It was an inviting little parcel, and I opened it instantly.

Inside, lying on a soft velvety cushion, was a gorgeous ring, shaped like a delicate buttercup with a tiny ruby nestling in the middle. I put on the ring and went over to give Grandpa Joe a huge thank-you hug. Then Mum said I could open my other presents.

I was so busy looking at all my lovely things that I wasn't really listening to my grandparents chatting away, but I realised that they were talking about how brains work.

When my brothers, Brad and Lee came in, I found myself saying: "Oh, I wish I could get inside a brain!"

"Whatever for, silly?" said Brad. "Nobody can do that!"

"But I would like to," I replied, giving my ring a comforting little twist.

All of a sudden everything went black.

I was spinning round and round, and then I landed with a bump.

When I opened my eyes I saw nothing but legs, brown wooden legs. Looking up I saw a huge birthday cake topped with gigantic candles. Brad and Lee loomed above me. I couldn't see their faces unless I lay on my back.

I HAD SHRUNK!

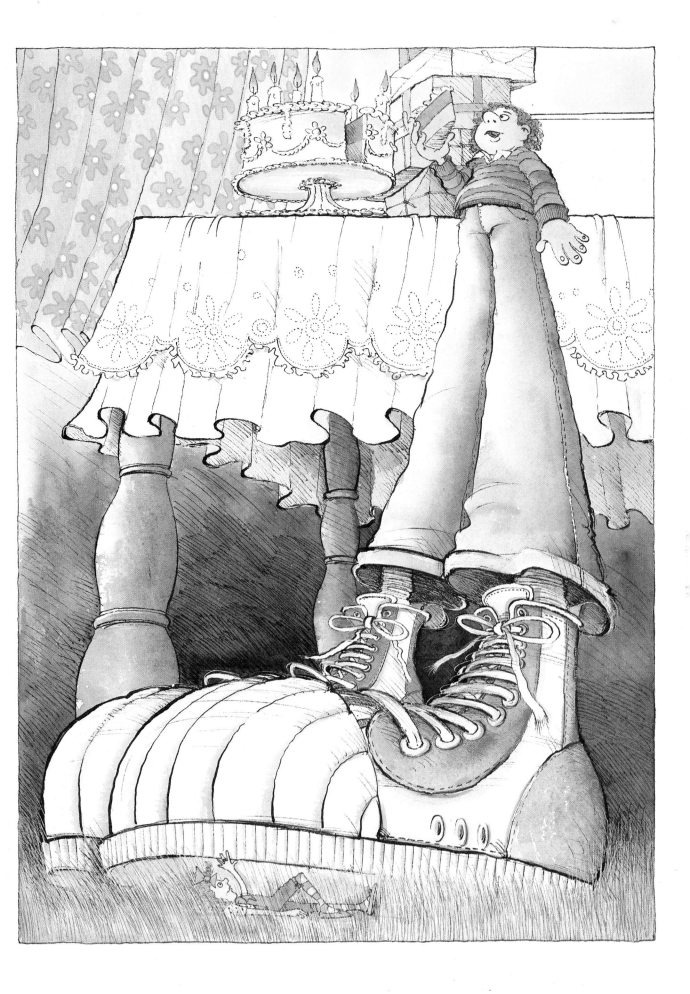

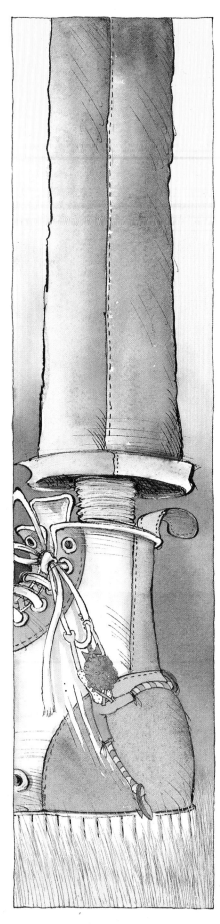
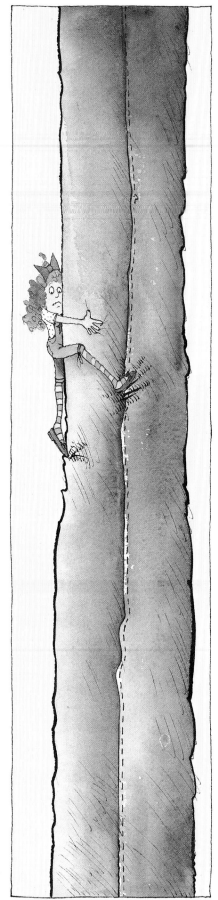
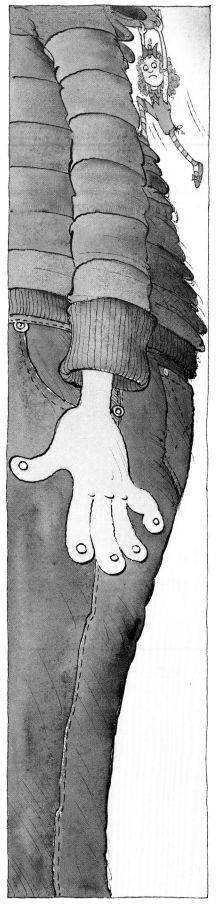

"Gosh!" I thought. "Now I'm small enough to get inside a brain."
Brad's brain! What would be the best way in? I didn't like the idea of
going through his nose or mouth . . . I would try his ears.

I darted from desk to table to sofa and finally reached Brad's foot.
Luckily he was wearing jeans and a woollen jumper, so I managed to
scramble up his legs quite easily. And no one spotted me on my woolly
climb – I was too small to be noticed.

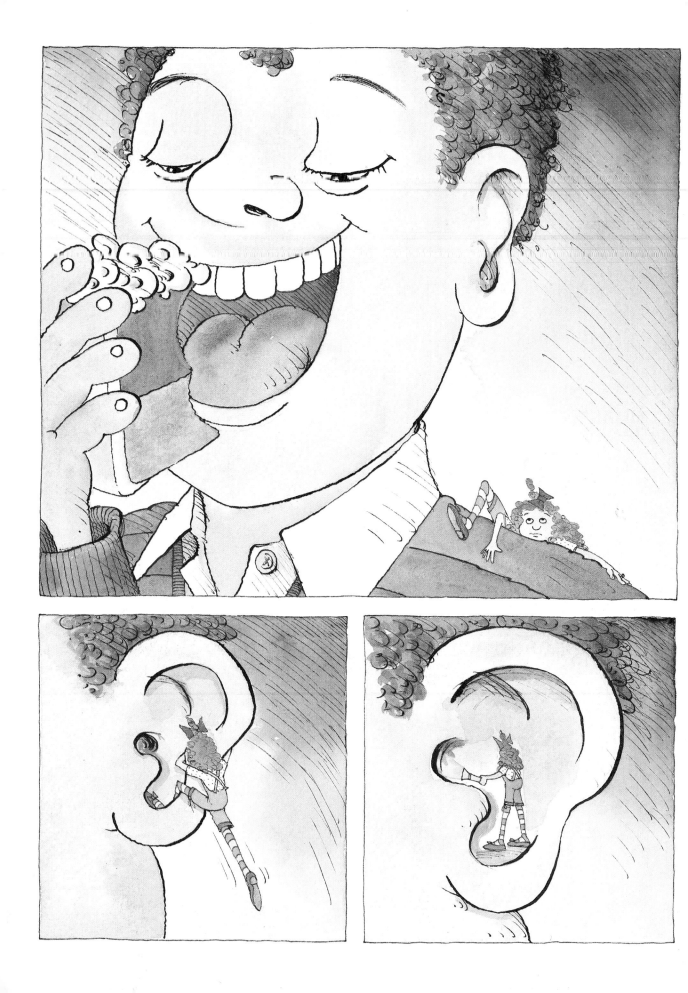

At last I reached the top. Puffing and panting, I stopped to catch my breath, perched on Brad's left shoulder. Then I made straight for his ear.

I peered inside. It was very dark. But I remembered I had put my new torch in my pocket. I switched it on and climbed into Brad's ear hole.

Twisting and turning round endless bends, I came at last to a closed door. I opened it.

And there, on the other side, sat a fat, jolly man. He was tinkering with a tin box with a dial on the side. He did not stop working with his miniature spanners, but he looked up.

"Hullo," I said politely. "My name's Kiki."

"How do you do?" replied the fat man. "I'm Mr Brainbox."

"What are you doing?" I asked.

"Just seeing what's the matter with this ear. It's not working too well."

"What are those levers marked *high* and *low*?" I asked.

"They help the ear hear high and low noises." Mr Brainbox smiled at me. "Would you like to see the rest of Brad's brain?"

"Oh, yes please," I answered.

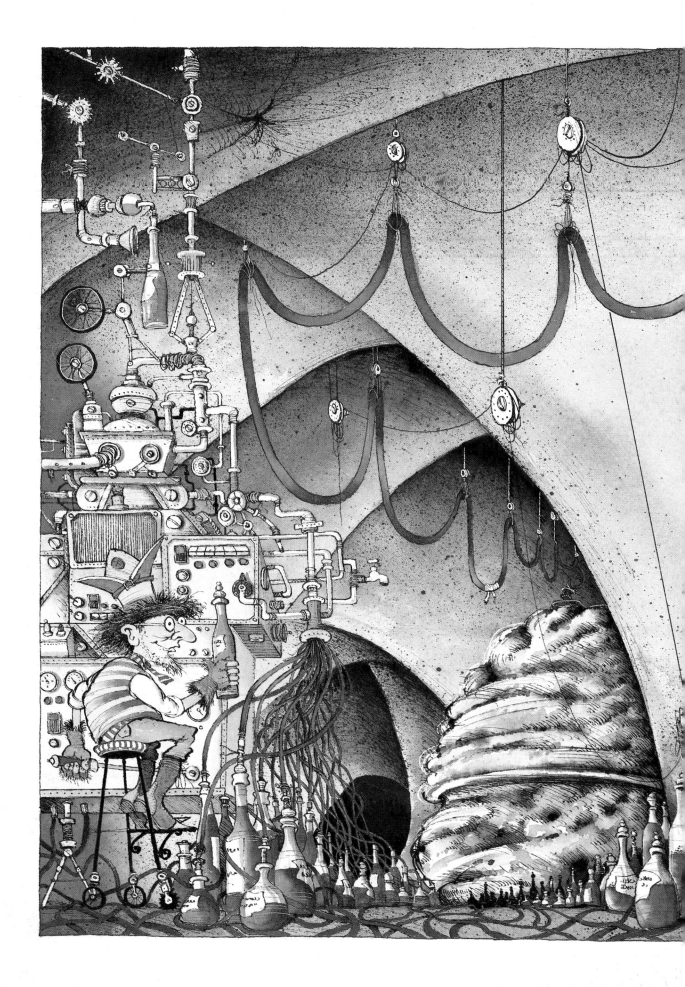

We walked along a long, dark passage until we came to a door marked "Ideas". Pushing it open, we walked in.

This room was bigger than Mr Brainbox's. Along one side were strange-looking machines attached to various pipes and bottles. A red fizzy liquid bubbled away in them. Lined up on many shelves were bottles of coloured liquids. All were labelled.

Peering through his spectacles at us was a wizened old man. He wore brown, fingerless gloves and he was holding a bottle of green liquid.

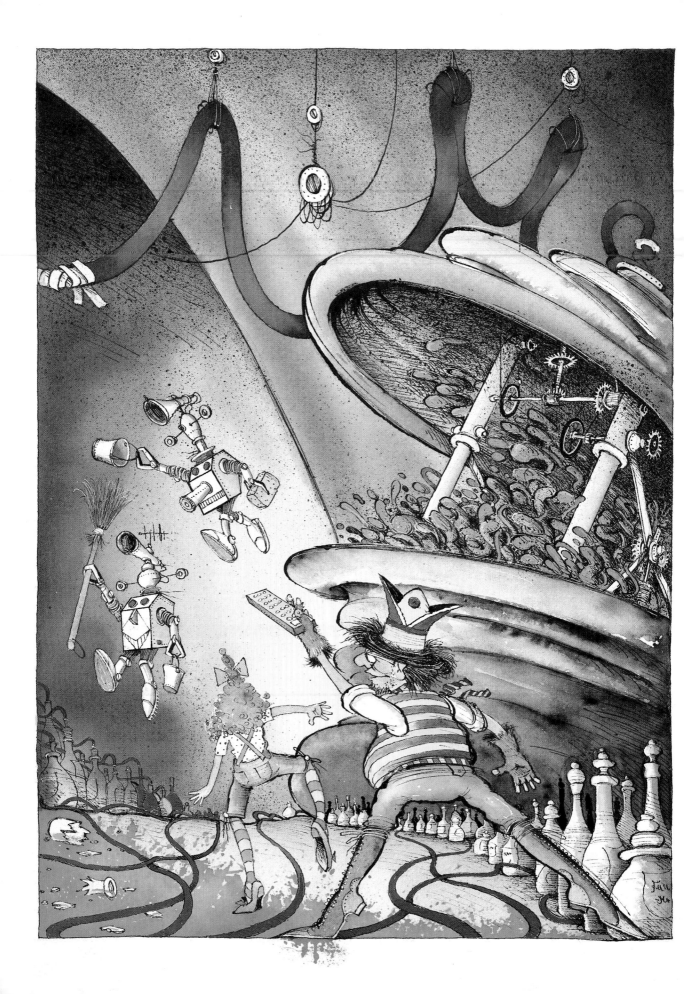

"What are you doing?" I asked curiously. The old man jumped, dropping his glass bottle. It smashed and liquid seeped across the floor.

"Drat it – that was a good Homework Dodge potion," muttered the old man. He picked up a key pad, pressed a button and the roof opened. Two little robots carrying sponges and buckets jumped down and began to clear up the mess.

Mr Brainbox took me over to read the labels on the bottles.

"Excuses for being late."

"Excuses for not doing homework."

"Ideas for not feeling well at school."

"Jokes to play on teachers."

And there were lots more. But I wanted to explore, so I said goodbye to the little old man, and followed Mr Brainbox out of the "Ideas" room.

Once more we were wandering down the long, dark passage. At last Mr Brainbox stopped and chose a room marked *Eyesight*. In the room were two men, one fat and one thin. Their skin was blue and they wore black clothes. Each was peering through a telescope.

"Of course," I murmured. Brad's eyes. Brad has peculiar eyes – especially his pupils. One is fat, the other is thin!

"Do speak to them, my dear," whispered Mr Brainbox.

"Hullo," I said.

"Hullo," they replied. "Can't look at you now, not until he's gone to sleep."

Now we were going through the door marked *Nerves*. I wished that Mr Brainbox hadn't opened that door.

We were surrounded by a horde of small round men. They were like hundreds of tiny bouncing balls and they had arms and legs sticking out all over the place.

A feather touched one of the nerves, and he yelled out.

"That couldn't have hurt you," I said scornfully.

"Oh, but it did. We nerves are so sensitive," he explained.

"Yes, we are, we are," chanted the other nerves.

They began to twitch up and down, and bounce against us. They had evil grins and clawing nails.

"Okay, okay," I said, grabbing Mr Brainbox by the hand, and we rushed out, slamming the door behind us.

"Oh, dear, oh dear, must you make such a noise?" said a very grumpy voice. And there, sitting in a deck chair, was a carbon copy of Brad's nose.

"Yes I must," I said huffily. "I'm not staying here to be insulted. How do I get out of here?"

"I couldn't tell you. All I do is sniff and smell. I haven't got a mind, you know."

"Then why aren't you where you should be, sniffing and smelling?" I asked.

"I'm on holiday," said the very stuffy nose.

"But what about Brad? What can he do without a nose?" I exclaimed.

"He can breathe. He can't smell, that's all. He's got a bit of a cold. You could try leaving by the mouth," added the nose. "Two doors down the corridor."

"I think you've had enough adventures for now," smiled Mr Brainbox. "Off you go – and goodbye until next time we meet."

"Goodbye Mr Brainbox. It was very kind of you to show me round."

I followed the nose's directions, and found myself at a door through which I could feel a brisk draught. I opened it and saw ahead of me a long red pipe. I began to walk down it. Suddenly I was feeling very tired. I stopped outside a narrow red door, opened it slowly – and twisted my ring. Soon I was spinning round and round.

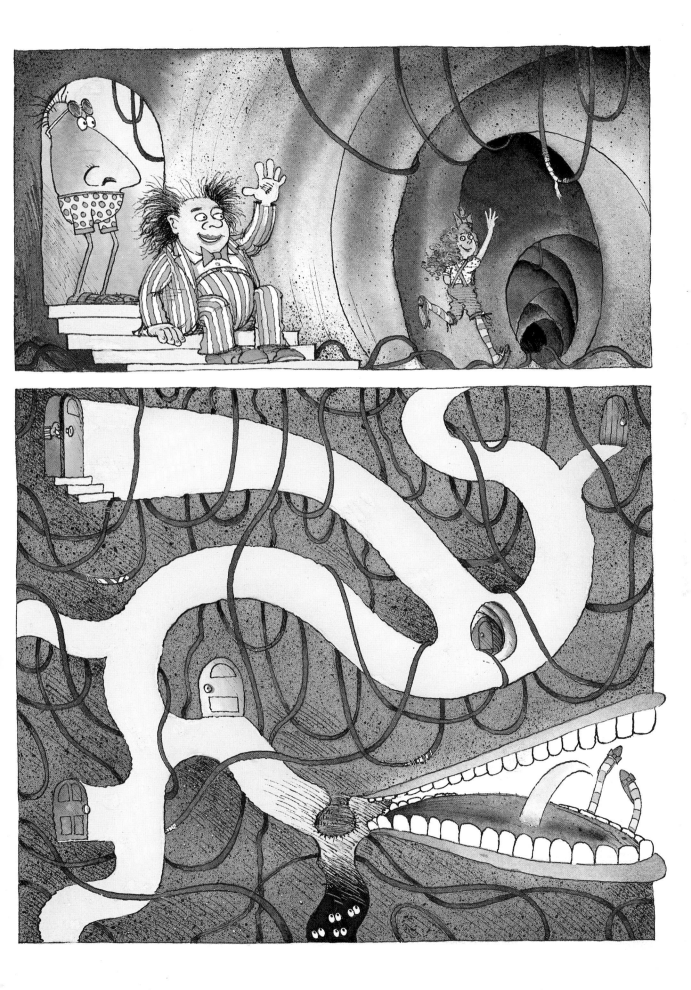

BUMP. I looked up, and saw Mum and Lee.

"Where am I? What happened?" I asked.

"Nothing, Kiki, you just fainted," my mother replied. "Too much excitement I expect."

So I hadn't been inside Brad's brain and met Mr Brainbox and Mr Ideas . . .

Then Brad rushed in shouting, "Mum, mum, I've got a terrible cold. My nose is all blocked up. And my left ear has been tickling most DREADFULLY."

And then, I knew it really had happened. I won't tell anyone or they'll say I was deaming. But I *KNOW* it happened. I hope you do too!